CALENDAR CLUB MYSTERIES™

The Case of the
THANKSGIVING THIEF

by **NANCY STAR**

Illustrated by
JAMES BERNARDIN

SCHOLASTIC INC.

New York   Toronto   London   Auckland   Sydney
Mexico City   New Delhi   Hong Kong   Buenos Aires

To JMac, with thanks for your friendship
— N. S.

For my niece, Claire Bernardin
— J. B.

ISBN 0-439-67261-9

12 11 10 9 8 7 6 5 4 3   6 7 8 9/0

Printed in the U.S.A.   40
First printing, November 2004

Book design by Jennifer Rinaldi Windau

CHAPTER ONE
THE HELP BOX

"I FOUND A NOTE!" Dottie Plum called out. "A note in our Help Box!"

The Help Box was right outside the Calendar Clubhouse front door. Casey Calendar had put it there after they solved their first case. Anyone in Fruitvale who needed help could slip a note inside.

Casey, Dottie, and Leon took turns checking the box every day.

But no one in town seemed to need any help. So the box stayed empty—until now.

Dottie ran into the clubhouse.

Casey and Leon dropped the pinecones and acorns they were sorting.

"I found our first note," Dottie said again.

She smiled. More than anything, Dottie liked to be first.

"What does it say?" Casey asked. "Did you read it yet? Did something happen in town?"

Dottie tore open the envelope. She pulled out a piece of paper and read:

Dear Calendar Club,
I need your help.
Please meet me
outside of Sweetie
Pie today at three.
From,
    a Calendar
    Club fan

"Our first fan!" Dottie said.

"Aren't we supposed to help your mother at Sweetie Pie today?" Leon asked Casey.

Sweetie Pie was the name of Mrs. Calendar's bakery.

Casey nodded. She had promised her mother they'd stop by after school to make Thanksgiving decorations for the front window.

The Fruitvale Public Library ran a contest

every Thanksgiving. Miss Webster was the librarian. She was in charge of picking the store window with the best Thanksgiving decorations.

This year, the Calendar Club was determined to help Sweetie Pie win first place.

"Do you think we have a fan club?" Casey asked. "With lots of members? And a president?"

"I think we should plan what we're going to do for the window," Leon said, changing the subject.

"What if we meet our fan first?" Casey asked. "And make decorations for the store after that?"

"Okay," Leon and Dottie agreed.

Dottie took her notebook out of her back pocket. She carried her notebook wherever she went. Inside, she kept lists. Her favorite list was of the weather.

Today, Dottie's weather list read, is forty-nine degrees and cloudy.

Dottie turned to the page that said: Thanksgiving Pinecone Turkey Supplies.

"But first let's check my list," Dottie said. She read the list out loud.

"Acorns, pinecones, red yarn, and orange pipe cleaners."

"These will make great turkey heads," Leon said as he picked up the acorns and stuffed them in his pockets.

"These pinecones are just the right shape for turkey bodies," Casey said. She put the pinecones in a small bag.

Dottie reached into her pocket. She pulled out a handful of red yarn.

"I have enough yarn to make turkey gobbles," she said.

"I have the pipe cleaners for the turkey feet," Casey said. "Let's get going!"

"Wait!" Dottie said. "There's something

we have to do first!"

She turned to a blank page in her book. She read as she made a new list:

"The Calendar Club Help Box. First note: Meet fan at 3:00 in front of Sweetie Pie."

"We'd better go," Casey said. "It's almost three now."

The three friends began their walk to town.

But when they got to the end of their block, they stopped.

Casey, Dottie, and Leon did not like to walk in front of the corner house on Daisy Lane.

It was a Calendar Club superstition.

The corner house was always dark. It was covered with ivy.

The woman who lived there was hardly ever home.

When she was home, she stayed inside.

Casey, Dottie, and Leon weren't totally sure the woman in the corner house disliked kids. But they were pretty sure. And they didn't want to take any chances.

"Ready?" Casey asked.

"Ready," Dottie and Leon said.

The three friends ran as fast as they could past the corner house.

"I wonder who left us the note," Leon said as he ran.

Casey and Dottie wondered the same thing.

CHAPTER TWO
PET ME!

IT ONLY TOOK ten minutes to walk to town. But when Casey and Dottie got there, Leon was nowhere to be seen.

This was nothing new.

Leon was a collector. He collected bottle caps, Popsicle sticks, and pumpkin stems. But his most important collection was of rocks that were in the shape of states. Leon hoped that someday he would have an entire map of the United States made out of rocks.

Leon spent a lot of time in the library. He liked to study maps and books about states. But he also liked to study rock piles, dirt mounds, and puddles. And studying the ground often made him late.

Casey and Dottie stopped in front of the new store, Pet Me. It was right next door to Sweetie Pie.

A sign in front of Pet Me said today was the grand opening.

The girls looked in the window. Inside were kittens chasing a toy mouse.

Leon ran over to join them.

"The pet store is finally open!" Leon exclaimed.

They watched as several kittens went to sleep.

"Want one?" a man asked as he walked out of the store.

A woman wearing a big hat came out of the store behind him.

The man carried a poster. It said, FREE TRAINING LESSON. THIS WEEK ONLY.

He taped the poster to the store window.

"I'm Mr. Cliff," the man said when he was done. "Would you like to come in and look around my store?"

"We can't," Dottie explained. "We're waiting for someone."

"Plus, we promised to help my mother with her Thanksgiving window decorations," Casey said.

"That's her store," Casey said. She pointed to Sweetie Pie.

"I heard about the Thanksgiving window contest," said Mr. Cliff. "I don't have time to enter this year. But don't be surprised if next year I put puppies wearing pilgrim hats in my window!"

The three friends were relieved that Pet Me wasn't going to be in the contest this year. They thought a window filled with puppies in pilgrim hats would be hard to beat!

The woman in the big hat cleared her throat.

"I'm sorry," Mr. Cliff said. "I forgot to introduce you. Do you know Mrs. Wagner? She just moved to town."

The three friends had never seen

Mrs. Wagner before. They would have remembered if they had.

Mrs. Wagner wore a red coat that had big wide pockets. She carried a big old brown leather purse. On her head was a wide-brimmed hat.

But that wasn't the most surprising thing about her.

A large blue-and-green parrot sat on Mrs. Wagner's hat. And a small gray-and-brown monkey sat inside her purse.

The monkey wore a bright red sweater. The sweater matched Mrs. Wagner's coat. It even had pockets.

The bird squawked. The monkey screeched.

"Quiet down, Beaky," Mrs. Wagner said. "Quiet down, Cappy."

The parrot and the monkey got quiet.

"They're very well trained," said Leon.

"Of course they are," Mrs. Wagner boasted. "That's because I'm a pet trainer. Do you have a pet?"

"No," said Leon. "I have allergies. I collect rocks, instead."

"I don't train rocks," Mrs. Wagner said. "I only train pets. And I'm having a Thanksgiving special." She pointed to the poster on the store window.

"I'm giving the first lesson for free," she said. "It's for this week only."

"That's very nice of you," said Mr. Cliff.

"Thank you," said Mrs. Wagner. "I think it's important to do something nice around Thanksgiving. I have so much to be thankful for. For one thing, I'm thankful people have pets."

She turned to Dottie. "Do you have a pet?"

Dottie nodded. "I have a cat named Ginger. But she's already trained."

"Her cat thinks she's a dog," Leon explained. "She likes to walk on a leash."

"Oh," said Mrs. Wagner. "Does she bark?"

"No," Dottie admitted.

"Would you like me to teach her to bark?" Mrs. Wagner's eyes sparkled. She liked the idea of teaching a cat to bark.

"No, thank you," Dottie said.

"She has a dog," Leon said, pointing to Casey. "Her dog thinks he's a cat."

"Oh," Mrs. Wagner said. "Does he purr?"

"No," Casey admitted.

"Would you like me to teach him to purr?" Mrs. Wagner asked.

"Can dogs really purr?" Casey asked.

"Of course," Mrs. Wagner said. "All they need is the right trainer." She smiled and looked at her watch.

"Oh, dear!" she sang out. "I have to go. I

can't be late. I've got an appointment with the librarian's cat."

"It's her second lesson," Mrs. Wagner explained. "The training hasn't worked yet. But I'm sure she'll get it."

"Get it!" the parrot squawked.

The monkey screeched.

Mrs. Wagner handed Casey a business card. It read: MRS. WANDA WAGNER. PET TRAINER.

"Don't forget my Thanksgiving special," Mrs. Wagner said. "I might be able to teach your dog to purr in one lesson. Or I can teach him to sing! Any dog can sing, if it has the right trainer."

Mrs. Wagner hurried to her next appointment.

Mr. Cliff said good-bye to the kids and went back inside his store.

Casey checked her watch. It was 3:15.

"Where is the person who left us the note?" she asked.

"Maybe we should check back in a little while," Dottie said. "It's getting late. Your mother is waiting for us."

"You're right," Casey said. "Let's go!"

Dottie and Casey went inside Sweetie Pie.

It took them a moment to realize Leon hadn't come in with them.

This was nothing new.

CHAPTER THREE
THE EARRINGS

MRS. CALENDAR WAS behind the counter helping some customers.

Casey ran over to her.

"Can Mrs. Wagner give our dog a free lesson?" she asked her mother.

"Who's Mrs. Wagner?" Mrs. Calendar asked.

"She's a new pet trainer," Casey said. "And the first lesson is free! It's a Thanksgiving special," she explained. "Mrs. Wagner loves Thanksgiving."

"Okay," Mrs. Calendar agreed. "I love Thanksgiving, too."

She went back to helping her customers.

Casey called Mrs. Wagner. She left a message saying her mother agreed to the free lesson.

Then Leon rushed in.

"Look at this," he said to his friends.

"Did you find a rock?" Casey asked. "Did you find a rock of Massachusetts?"

Leon really wanted to find a rock of Massachusetts. His Grandpa Jeff was from Massachusetts. And Grandpa Jeff always told good stories about his home state.

Grandpa Jeff was a collector, too. He collected pictures of the *Mayflower*. That was the ship the Pilgrims sailed on to America.

Leon and Grandpa Jeff had just finished making a model ship of the *Mayflower*. And Mrs. Calendar agreed to let the three friends use it in the Thanksgiving window display.

Leon opened his hand.

The girls leaned over to take a look.

"It's not really the right shape for Massachusetts," Leon said.

"Could it be Alaska?" Casey asked.

"Alaska does have a long skinny bottom just like this rock," Leon said. "But the rest of the shape doesn't look like Alaska to me."

Dottie looked more closely. It was a very unusual rock. It was pale pink. It was very smooth. And it was shiny.

"That will be enough," a man's voice boomed out.

The three friends looked up.

A man and a woman stood at the counter. Mrs. Calendar was filling up a box with brownies for them.

Mrs. Calendar was famous for her chocolate cream pie, strawberry shortcake, and sugar donuts. But she was most famous for her double-fudge brownies.

The woman took the box.

"Come along, dear," she said to the man. "We have to pick out our puppy."

"I thought we were getting a kitten," the man said.

The woman disagreed. "No," she said. "We decided on a puppy. Remember?"

She left before the man could answer.

But the man didn't follow her. He stopped to stare at Mrs. Calendar's apron.

Mrs. Calendar always wore an apron in her store. And she always wore a pin on her apron. She wore different pins for different holidays. Today she was wearing a turkey pin, for Thanksgiving.

"Your pin is very unusual," the man said.

"Thank you," Mrs. Calendar said.

The man leaned closer to get a better look.

"Just as I thought," he said. "The turkey's eyes are made of red glass." He sounded disappointed. He didn't sound very interested in a turkey pin that had eyes made of glass.

The man walked past Leon and stopped. He stared at the rock in Leon's open hand.

"What do you have there?" the man asked.

Leon closed his hand. "Nothing," he said.

"It's just a rock," Dottie said.

"Just a rock?" the man repeated.

"He collects rocks," Dottie said.

The door opened.

"Come on," the woman yelled at him. "We have to pick out our puppy."

The man muttered something to himself and left the store.

The three friends exchanged a look. There was something about the man they didn't like.

Mrs. Calendar interrupted them.

"Did you get the note I put in your Help Box?" she asked.

"That note was from you?" Casey asked. She sounded disappointed. "We thought a real person wrote that note."

Mrs. Calendar laughed. "I *am* a real

person," she said. "And I do need your help. I made a big batch of brownies for Mr. Cliff's new store. But I'm too busy to deliver them.

"I always get busy with special orders the week before Thanksgiving," Mrs. Calendar explained. "But I realized the Calendar Club could help me out. You could deliver the brownies to Mr. Cliff."

"Can we take them over after we work on the window decorations?" Casey asked.

"Sure," said Mrs. Calendar.

She started arranging the brownies on a tray.

Dottie, Casey, and Leon planned how to decorate the window.

Dottie got started first. She painted a border of pilgrim hats along the top.

Casey worked on making ocean waves

out of blue construction paper. She taped paper to the bottom of the window. Everyone agreed that it really looked like the ocean.

Leon set up the model of the *Mayflower*.

"Now let's make the pinecone turkeys," Casey said.

The three friends went to the back room. Mrs. Calendar had set up a work-table for them there.

They had finished six pinecone turkeys when they heard something strange.

It was coming from the front of the store.

"It sounds like a radio stuck between stations," Leon said.

The friends stopped what they were doing. They listened. They heard a crackling sound.

"It sounds like a walkie-talkie," Dottie said.

They went to the doorway.

They saw Officer Gill holding a walkie-talkie to his ear. Then he hooked it back on his belt.

He said something quietly to Mrs. Calendar and hurried out the door.

Casey, Dottie, and Leon ran to the front of the shop.

Dottie got to Mrs. Calendar first.

"What happened?" Dottie asked.

"Why did Officer Gill rush out?" Casey asked.

"He had to go see Mrs. Jackson," Mrs. Calendar explained. "Her pearl earrings are missing. And that's not all that's missing."

"What else is missing?" Casey asked.

Mrs. Calendar turned to Dottie. "Officer Gill told me your uncle called. He wanted to know if anyone found his watch."

"Uncle Eddy lost his watch?" Dottie asked.

"It's missing," Mrs. Calendar said.

Dottie took out her notebook and started a new list. She wrote:

Missing Jewelry:
Mrs. Jackson's pearl earrings
Uncle Eddy's watch

"And Miss Webster, the librarian, lost her cat's silver collar," said Mrs. Calendar.

Dottie added Miss Webster's silver cat collar to her list.

The three friends went back to work on their pinecone turkeys. But they weren't thinking about the Thanksgiving window contest anymore. They were thinking about the missing jewelry.

CHAPTER FOUR
A NECKLACE NEXT!

DOTTIE, CASEY, AND LEON couldn't stop thinking about the missing jewelry. They were thinking about it when they brought Mr. Cliff the tray of brownies.

Mr. Cliff took the tray. He put it on his desk.

"Thank you," he said. "Thank you very much."

He seemed distracted. He patted his pockets.

"Where is it?" he asked.

"Where is what?" Casey asked.

"I know I put it on my desk," Mr. Cliff said.

Mr. Cliff picked up some papers. He looked underneath them. He looked underneath his desk. He looked on the floor.

"It's gone," said Mr. Cliff.

"What did you lose?" Casey asked.

"We're good at finding things," Dottie said.

"The pendant from my wife's necklace," Mr. Cliff said.

"What does it look like?" Leon asked.

"It looks broken," Mr. Cliff said. "I promised to give it to the jeweler today. I wanted it fixed by Thanksgiving. I put it on my desk so I wouldn't forget. And now it isn't there."

Dottie took out her notebook. She turned to the page that said, Missing Jewelry.

She wrote:

Mr. Cliff's broken necklace.

"I couldn't have lost it," Mr. Cliff said. "I must have left it at home."

"Are you sure?" Casey asked.

"A lot of jewelry has disappeared," Leon said.

Dottie read Mr. Cliff her list:

Missing Jewelry:
Mrs. Jackson's pearl earrings
Uncle Eddy's watch
Miss Webster's cat's silver collar
Mr. Cliff's broken necklace

"And that's just what we know so far," Leon added.

"No. I left it at home. I'm sure of it," Mr. Cliff said. "At least I think I'm sure."

"Okay," Casey said. "But let us know if you don't find it."

The three friends left the store and set out for home.

When they got to Daisy Lane, they crossed the street to avoid the corner house.

But Leon stopped. "Look!" he said.

Casey and Dottie looked.

A man and woman were standing in front of the ivy-covered corner house. It was the same man and woman who had been in Mrs. Calendar's store!

"That's the man who asked your mother about her pin," Leon said.

"How does he know the woman in the corner house?" Casey asked.

The man rang the bell. He held a small pet carrier. It was hard to tell whether it held a puppy or a kitten.

The three friends watched from behind a tree. The front door of the corner house opened.

"She's home!" Leon said.

"Want to see what we got today?" the man asked in his booming voice.

The couple went into the house. The front door slammed.

"I knew those two seemed strange," Dottie said.

They waited to see what would happen next.

Then Casey looked down the street. She saw someone waiting in front of her house.

"It's Mrs. Wagner!" she said. "I forgot that my mother said she called back and made an appointment with us!"

The three friends raced down the street to meet the pet trainer.

Dottie got there first.

CHAPTER FIVE
FREE LESSON

MRS. WAGNER WORE her red coat. On her
head was her wide-brimmed hat. Beaky,
her parrot, sat on top of her hat. Cappy,
her monkey, peeked out from inside her big,
brown purse.

"Sorry we're late," Casey said.

"No problem," Mrs. Wagner said. "I love
the fresh air. That's why I believe in training
animals outdoors. Animals don't like house
air. They like fresh air. Don't you?"

Just then, Mrs. Calendar drove up. She
parked in front of the house.

"Just in time," Mrs. Wagner said. "Do
you have a backyard?"

"Yes," Casey said.

"Then, let's go," Mrs. Wagner said. "You
know what they say. An animal that's well-
trained outside will be well-trained inside."

Casey, Dottie, and Leon had never heard anyone say that. But they smiled politely anyway.

Mrs. Wagner marched to the backyard.

Dottie, Casey, and Leon went into the house to get Silky, the dog.

Mrs. Calendar opened the back door and let everyone out.

Silky was the last one to leave the house. But as soon as he came out, Beaky, the parrot, flew in.

Cappy, the monkey, ran after Beaky.

"Those two just love giving themselves house tours!" said Mrs. Wagner.

She turned to Mrs. Calendar. "Do you mind? Cappy's a very well-trained monkey."

Mrs. Calendar looked a little worried. She didn't like the idea of a monkey in her house, even a well-trained monkey. But she didn't want to miss hearing Silky purr.

"I guess it's all right," Mrs. Calendar said. She sat down on the back steps.

Mrs. Wagner turned toward the dog.

"You must be Silky," she said.

Silky had wavy white hair and big, brown eyes.

"What a cute little dog," Mrs. Wagner said. "Come here!"

Silky ran over to Mrs. Wagner.

"Silky doesn't usually do that," Casey said, surprised. "He usually just blinks at people when they call his name."

"All animals like me," Mrs. Wagner said. She took a treat out of her pocket.

"Silky, sit," said Mrs. Wagner.

Silky sat. Mrs. Wagner gave him the treat.

"Silky never eats when company is over," Casey said.

"Silky understands that I'm not company," Mrs. Wagner said.

"Now," she said, "let's show Silky how to purr, shall we? Who knows how to purr?"

"Not me," Casey said. She looked at Dottie.

"Not me," Dottie said. She looked at Leon.

"I collect rocks," Leon said.

"Then I suppose I'll have to show him how to do it," said Mrs. Wagner.

"Silky," Mrs. Wagner said. "Listen to me. I'm going to purr with you."

Mrs. Wagner made a low, humming sound.

The three friends didn't think it sounded like purring. But they didn't say anything. They were too busy trying not to laugh.

Mrs. Wagner noticed. "If you're not serious, it won't work," she said. She started to hum again.

Just then they heard a tap coming from inside the house.

"That must be Beaky," Mrs. Wagner said. "I guess the house tour is over."

Casey opened the door. Beaky flew out. The parrot settled on top of Mrs. Wagner's hat.

Cappy ran out of the house next. He hopped into Mrs. Wagner's big, brown purse.

"I don't think Silky wants to purr today," Mrs. Wagner said.

"Can you teach him to sing?" Casey asked.

"Of course," Mrs. Wagner said. "I can teach any dog to sing. But we're done for today. If you'd like another lesson, just give me a call."

Mrs. Wagner marched down the driveway. Cappy stared at the three friends from inside the large, brown purse.

"I'm not allergic to monkeys," Leon said when Mrs. Wagner was gone, "but I wish I was. That monkey gives me the creeps."

"Me, too," Dottie said.

Silky barked.

The three friends laughed.

"I'm going inside," Mrs. Calendar said. "I have to review tomorrow's special orders for the bakery."

Mrs. Calendar went in the house. A moment later she came out looking very upset.

"What's wrong?" Casey asked.

"I'm not sure," Mrs. Calendar said, "but I think I lost my ring."

CHAPTER SIX

A NEW NOTE

CASEY, DOTTIE, AND LEON helped Mrs. Calendar look for her ring. But they couldn't find it.

"Maybe I wasn't wearing it," Mrs. Calendar said.

The three friends weren't convinced. They went to the clubhouse to talk about it.

Dottie and Casey went inside first. Leon stopped to check the Help Box.

A moment later he called out, "There's a new note!"

He ran into the clubhouse holding it.

He read it out loud:

"Dear Calendar Club,

"I need your help. Please meet me at the playground at 3:30 tomorrow afternoon. I'll be on the third swing."

It was signed WB.

"Who is WB?" Dottie wondered.

"I have an idea," Leon said.

"Who?" Casey asked. "Is WB someone we know?"

But Leon wouldn't say.

The next day at 3:30, they hurried to the playground.

Dottie got there first.

"No one is on the swings," Dottie said.

Leon looked relieved. But not for long.

"Oh, no," he said. "Look!"

Casey and Dottie looked. Two boys hopped off their bikes. They didn't bother with their kickstands. They didn't care when their bikes crashed to the ground.

It was Warren Bunn and Derek Fleck.

Warren was a boy in their grade who was a bully and proud of it. Derek was his best friend.

Warren and Derek walked toward the

swings. They kicked up clumps of grass. They got on the swings.

Dottie frowned.

Warren Bunn was on the third swing.

"Is he WB?" Casey asked. "Did Warren Bunn leave us that note?"

"Why did it have to be him?" asked Leon.

Dottie thought about it for a moment. It didn't make sense.

"Why would Warren Bunn want our help?" she asked.

"You're right," Leon said. "Warren Bunn doesn't think he needs help. Not from us."

"I'll just have to ask him," Casey said.

Casey walked right up to where Warren was swinging.

Warren laughed and made his swing go faster so it would hit her.

But Casey got out of the way in time.

"Lookie, lookie here," Warren said. "It's Fruitvale's shortest detectives."

"Hey, Leon," Derek called out. "Find any more rocks?"

"Because if you ever run out," Warren added, "you can always use the ones in your head."

The two bullies laughed so hard they snorted and closed their eyes.

When Warren opened his eyes, two girls were standing in front of him.

He had never seen these girls before.

The girls were older. They were from the fifth grade. They didn't look like they thought Warren was very funny.

"It's my turn," one of the girls told him. "You have to get off."

Warren didn't like it when people told him what to do.

"This swing is taken," Warren said. But he didn't sound completely sure.

"Pardon me?" the girl said. She was very tall. Her black hair was perfectly straight.

"I said this swing is taken," Warren said. But this time he sounded even less sure.

Warren got off the swing. He stood in front of it. He crossed his arms and squinted. He tried to make his face look tough.

The tall girl smiled.

"Thank you," she said.

She walked past Warren and hopped up on his swing.

"You might want to move," she said politely.

She started swinging. "I don't want to kick you. By accident," she added.

Warren looked over at Derek. He wasn't sure what to do.

Derek stared back.

"What's your problem?" Warren asked Derek.

"Me?" Derek said. "I don't have a problem."

"Then why are you still on that stupid swing?" Warren asked. "Come on. We got to go."

"Where?" Derek asked.

Warren glared. "You know where," he said.

Warren stormed over to his bike. He picked it up.

"I'll go without you," Warren snapped. He started to ride away.

"Wait up," Derek called after him. He jumped off his swing. He ran over to his bike.

"Where are we going?" Derek yelled. He started to pedal toward Warren. He pedaled as fast as he could.

Warren and Derek left the park.

The fifth-grade girls laughed.

Leon, Casey, and Dottie stared. They had never seen anyone laugh at Warren Bunn before.

The tall girl called over to them.

"Which one of you is Casey Calendar?" she asked.

"I am," Casey said. She raised her hand.

"I'm Wendy Block," the tall girl said.

"I'm Kathryn," Wendy's friend said.

Suddenly, Dottie noticed something. "You're on the third swing," she said to Wendy.

Wendy nodded.

Casey's eyes widened. "Are you WB?" she asked. "Are you the one who left the note in the Help Box?"

"Yes," Wendy said. She got off the swing. She looked around.

"Is there somewhere we can go to talk?" Wendy asked.

"How about our clubhouse?" Casey suggested.

Wendy and Kathryn nodded.

They walked quickly to Casey's house.

At the corner of Daisy Lane, Casey, Dottie, and Leon looked both ways. Then they crossed the street.

"We don't like that house," Dottie explained.

"The woman who lives there is hardly ever home," Leon added.

"And when she is, she isn't very nice," Casey said.

Just then the front door of the corner house opened.

Casey, Leon, and Dottie didn't wait to find out if the woman had heard them. They ran as fast as they could to Casey's driveway.

Wendy and Kathryn followed.

Dottie got to the clubhouse first.

CHAPTER SEVEN
THE BRACELET

THEY SAT IN THE MIDDLE of the clubhouse floor.

Dottie had her pen in her hand.

"Do you promise you won't tell anyone?" Kathryn asked.

"We promise," Dottie said. "I'm just taking notes because it helps us figure things out."

"Okay," Wendy said. "The problem is my bracelet. I got it for my birthday from Caroline," Wendy said.

"Who's Caroline?" Casey asked.

"She's the most popular girl in fifth grade," Kathryn explained.

Kathryn pointed to a charm bracelet on her wrist. "She gives everyone she likes charm bracelets."

"Let me guess," Leon said to Wendy. "Is your bracelet missing?"

Wendy looked surprised.

"How did you know?" Wendy asked.

"It's my turn to guess," Casey said. "Did you leave it somewhere? And then it disappeared?"

"Yes," Wendy and Kathryn said together.

"How did you know?" Wendy asked again.

Dottie added bracelet to her list of missing jewelry.

"Where did you leave it?" Casey asked.

"I put it on my kitchen counter," Wendy said. "And half an hour later it was gone."

"Why did you take it off?" Casey asked.

"Mrs. Wagner told me to," Wendy said.

Now it was Casey, Dottie, and Leon who were surprised.

"Mrs. Wagner was at your house?" Casey asked.

Wendy nodded. "We were in my backyard," she said. "Training my puppy."

"He's cute, but he doesn't listen," Kathryn said.

"Mrs. Wagner is a very good dog trainer," Wendy said. "She told me dogs like to chew on jewelry. So I put my bracelet in the house. But when the lesson was over, it was gone."

"Caroline will never believe you lost it," Kathryn said.

Dottie said, "I don't believe you lost it, either."

CHAPTER EIGHT
NOTHING IS LOST!

THE THREE FRIENDS RAN all the way to Mrs. Calendar's store.

"We don't think you lost your ring!" Casey told her mother.

"We don't think Uncle Eddy lost his watch," Dottie said.

"We don't think Miss Webster lost her cat's silver collar," Leon said.

"What do you mean?" asked Mrs. Calendar.

"We think your ring was stolen," Leon said.

"We think all the missing jewelry was stolen," Dottie said. "And we think we know who stole it."

Mrs. Calendar didn't ask any more questions. This sounded serious.

She called Officer Gill. He promised to come right over.

Mrs. Calendar hung up the phone and picked up a tray of brownies.

"Why don't you have a snack while we wait?" she said. "I made these brownies just for you. It's my way of saying thank you for the Thanksgiving window."

They had never seen brownies like these before. They were huge. And Mrs. Calendar had painted a pilgrim's hat with butter-cream frosting on top of each one.

"Mmm," Casey said as she took a bite out of her brownie. "These are the best double-fudge brownies you've ever made."

"Mmm," Dottie said. "These are the best brownies anyone has ever made."

Leon stared at his brownie. Then he stared at the window display.

"Leon," Mrs. Calendar said. "Are you okay? Why aren't you eating your brownie?"

Leon took the pink rock out of his pocket. He held it up next to his brownie.

His friends saw it at once.

"That rock looks just like a pilgrim's hat," Dottie said.

"A perfect pilgrim's hat!" Casey said.

Leon held the rock for a minute longer. Then he turned it over.

"Except I don't think it's an ordinary rock," he said. "Look!"

Leon ran his fingers over a set of bumps on the back of the rock.

"I think this rock is a pendant from a necklace," Leon said.

"Is it part of the necklace Mr. Cliff lost?" Casey asked.

"I think it's from Mrs. Cliff's necklace," Leon said. "But I don't think Mr. Cliff lost it."

CHAPTER NINE

THAT'S IT!

DOTTIE, CASEY, AND LEON ran inside Pet Me.

Mr. Cliff was just finishing up with a customer.

The customer turned around. It was the man with the booming voice.

"Hello," Mr. Cliff said to Dottie, Casey, and Leon. "This is my friend, Mr. Thomas."

"Mr. Thomas is a jeweler," Mr. Cliff explained. "He's the person who was going to fix my wife's necklace."

"I remember you," Mr. Thomas said to Leon. "Aren't you the one who had that pink stone?"

"I still have it," Leon said.

He handed the stone to Mr. Cliff. "But I think it belongs to you."

"That's from my wife's necklace!" Mr.

Cliff said. "Where did you find it?"

"I'll show you," Leon said.

They all followed Leon outside.

"I found it the same day you lost it," Leon said. "But I didn't know it was part of a necklace. I thought it was just a rock."

"I can understand that," Mr. Thomas said. "Some rocks are very beautiful."

"But how did it get outside?" asked Mr. Cliff. "I left it right on my desk."

"Did you ever think someone might have taken it?" Casey asked.

"Why would someone take it?" asked Mr. Cliff. "It didn't cost much. It's valuable to Mrs. Cliff and me because I bought it on our first vacation. We went to Massachusetts," he said. "Have you ever been to Massachusetts?"

"No," Leon said. "But my Grandpa Jeff is from Massachusetts."

Leon saw something interesting on the

ground. He bent down and picked it up.

"I found it!" he said. "I found a rock that looks like Massachusetts!"

Casey and Dottie looked at the rock in Leon's hands.

"It's perfect!" Casey exclaimed, proud that she recognized the shape.

"This is exactly where I found the pilgrim hat stone," Leon said. He pointed to a pile of rocks and dirt.

"But how did it get there?" Mr. Cliff wondered out loud.

"We think it was stolen," Dottie said. "By a jewel thief."

"A jewel thief?" said Mr. Thomas. "Officer Gill told me to be on the lookout for a jewel thief."

"Mr. Cliff," said Casey. "Was anyone with you when the necklace disappeared?"

Mr. Cliff thought for a moment. "No," he said.

He thought some more.

"Wait a minute," said Mr. Cliff. "Mrs. Wagner was in the store. She came to introduce herself and to drop off her poster."

"Mrs. Wagner!" the three friends called out together.

"But Mrs. Wagner couldn't have stolen the necklace," said Mr. Cliff. "I would have seen her take it. Besides, if she stole it, why would it have ended up on the ground?"

"Maybe she dropped it," Leon suggested.

Dottie took out her notebook. She opened to the page that said, Missing Jewelry.

"We know Mrs. Wagner was in Wendy Block's backyard when Wendy's bracelet disappeared," Dottie said.

"And she was in my backyard when my

mother's ring vanished," Casey said. "But she wasn't in the house," Casey added. "And the ring was in the house. So how can she be the thief?"

"Too bad we can't talk this over with Beaky," Leon said.

"That's it!" Dottie said.

"The bird!" Casey said.

"The bird?" Mr. Cliff said.

"And the monkey!" Leon said.

"The monkey?" Mr. Thomas said.

The three friends smiled.

It was time to set a trap for Mrs. Wagner and her animal gang.

CHAPTER TEN

THE TRAP

MRS. WAGNER WAS DELIGHTED to come back to Casey's house to teach Silky to sing.

As usual, she wore her red coat. She wore her big, brimmed hat. Her parrot sat on top of her hat. Her monkey peeked out from her brown leather purse.

Casey brought Silky outside through the back door. Mrs. Calendar followed them.

Beaky immediately flew off of Mrs. Wagner's hat.

"Poor Beaky," Mrs. Wagner said. "She always gets nervous around Thanksgiving. I keep telling her that turkeys are the ones who need to be nervous. Not parrots!"

Mrs. Wagner sighed. "Would you mind if Beaky waited in your house?"

"Not at all," Casey said.

Casey held open the back door. Beaky flew inside. The monkey followed.

"That monkey loves house tours," said Mrs. Wagner. "Do you mind?"

"Not at all," Casey repeated.

"I love house tours, too," Dottie said. "I think I'll join them."

"I think I'll go inside with them," Leon said.

"So will I," Casey said. Casey smiled sweetly at Mrs. Wagner. "You don't mind, do you?"

"I most certainly do," Mrs. Wagner said. "I came here to give your dog a lesson. And I need everyone to help."

"Do you need my help, too?" a voice called from the kitchen.

"You didn't tell me anyone was inside the house," Mrs. Wagner said, scowling.

"That's because it's not just anyone," Casey said.

Officer Gill walked out of the house. He

held the monkey in his arms.

"Does this belong to you?" he asked.

"Yes, he does," said Mrs. Wagner.

The monkey screeched.

"Quiet down, Cappy," Mrs. Wagner said.

Cappy got quiet. He tried to wriggle out of Officer Gill's arms. But Officer Gill held tight.

Officer Gill reached into the monkey's pocket. He pulled out a gold necklace.

"Does this belong to you, too?" Officer Gill asked.

"That's my mother's necklace," Casey said.

"Really?" Mrs. Wagner sang out. "How did your mother's necklace get into my monkey's pocket?"

"Mrs. Wagner," Officer Gill said, "would you please remove your hat?"

"Most certainly not!" said Mrs. Wagner. "I always wear my hat."

A sharp tap on the back door interrupted them.

Beaky wanted to come out.

Casey opened the door. The parrot flew out of the house.

"Get it," Beaky squawked as he flew over Mrs. Wagner's head.

Something shiny dropped from the bird's claw into Mrs. Wagner's hat.

The monkey sprang out of Officer Gill's arms. It ran to Mrs. Wagner and scampered into her bag.

The monkey made Mrs. Wagner lose her balance. Luckily, she didn't fall.

But her hat did. It sailed through the air. And it settled slowly on the ground.

The three friends stared down in amazement. The hat brim was filled with jewelry.

"There's Uncle Eddy's watch," Dottie said.

"And my mother's ring," Casey said.

"And Wendy's charm bracelet," Leon said.

"And Miss Webster's silver cat collar," said Mrs. Calendar.

"Do you mind telling us why you were walking around with all that jewelry in your hat?" Officer Gill asked Mrs. Wagner.

"I was going to the pawn shop to sell it. Then she called." Mrs. Wagner pointed to Casey. "So I figured I'd stop here first."

Officer Gill scooped up the jewelry and put it inside a plastic bag. Then he handed Mrs. Wagner her hat.

"You can wear it," said Officer Gill. "For now."

Mrs. Wagner's shoulders sagged. She put her hat back on her head.

Beaky hopped onto her hat. Cappy jumped into her purse.

Officer Gill led them to his police car and drove Mrs. Wagner and her gang away.

CHAPTER ELEVEN
GIVING THANKS

MISS WEBSTER, the librarian, walked from store to store. Dottie, Casey, and Leon followed her.

Miss Webster carried a pad of paper. She made notes on what she saw.

Dottie carried her notebook. She jotted down what she saw, too.

The first stop was the corner hardware store. The window of the hardware store had a painting of Squanto and Samoset. They were both Native Americans who Dottie, Casey, and Leon learned about in school.

The three friends thought it was a great idea to put a painting of Squanto and Samoset in a Thanksgiving window. They thought it might even be a winning idea.

Miss Webster made a note on her list.

Dottie made a note in her notebook.

The next stop was the grocery store. The grocery store window was almost completely covered with Indian corn.

Dottie, Casey, and Leon thought putting Indian corn in the window was a great idea, too.

Miss Webster wrote a note on her list and Dottie made a note in her notebook.

The last store they went to was Sweetie Pie. Miss Webster stared at the Sweetie Pie window for a long time.

"I made the ship with my Grandpa Jeff," Leon said.

"It's supposed to be the *Mayflower*," Dottie added.

"I can tell," Miss Webster said. She wrote some notes on her list. Then she said, "That's it. I'm done."

"Can you tell us who won the contest?" Casey asked.

"You'll have to wait until tomorrow," Miss Webster said. "I'll announce the winner at the Fruitvale Thanksgiving Lunch."

The Fruitvale Library had a Thanksgiving lunch every year. Everyone in town came to the feast.

This year, Miss Webster had asked Dottie, Casey, and Leon to plan the menu.

The three friends made sure the feast included some food that was probably eaten at the very first Thanksgiving, like turkey and corn.

But they also made sure it included some food that wasn't eaten then, like Uncle Eddy's pumpkin pies and Mrs. Calendar's double-fudge brownies with pilgrim hats painted on top.

Leon's Grandpa Jeff brought his collection of pictures of the *Mayflower*. Miss Webster hung them on the wall in the main room of the library. That's where the feast was served.

"Can I have everyone's attention, please?" the librarian said when all the neighbors sat down.

"Thanksgiving is almost here," Miss Webster said. "And I'd like each of us to take a moment to think about something we are thankful for."

After a moment of silence, Miss Webster said, "I would like to say that I am thankful you all are here. And Officer Gill would like to give thanks for something else."

Officer Gill stood up.

"On behalf of the Fruitvale Police Department," he said, "I want to thank our young detectives."

He pointed to the three friends. "Dottie Plum, Casey Calendar, and Leon Spector."

Dottie, Casey, and Leon beamed.

The crowd clapped.

"Thank you for helping us get back our missing jewelry," said Officer Gill.

Miss Webster lifted up her cat and pointed to the silver collar.

Wendy Block held up her arm. Everyone admired her charm bracelet.

Uncle Eddy held up his watch.

Mrs. Jackson turned her head to show her pearl earrings.

Mrs. Calendar raised her hand and pointed to her ring.

"I'm happy to report the jewel thief is in jail," Officer Gill went on.

A loud screech interrupted him. Everyone turned toward Mr. Cliff. He was holding the monkey in his arms.

There was a loud squawk. Beaky, the parrot, settled on Mr. Cliff's shoulder.

"Mr. Cliff is going to make sure the rest of her gang stays out of trouble," said Officer Gill.

"Who gets to keep the monkey?" shouted Warren Bunn.

Lots of children shouted "Me!"

Lots of parents shouted "No!"

"Beaky and Cappy will live with me," said Mr. Cliff.

"Aw," said Warren. "I always wanted a monkey."

"I have a question for Casey," called a voice from the crowd.

It was Warren Bunn's little sister, Emma.

"How did you know who stole the jewelry?" Emma asked.

"We just thought about the clues," Dottie said.

"You can read all about it in the next edition of *The Monthly Calendar*," Casey said.

"But I can't read," Emma said.

"Your brother will read it to you," said Mrs. Bunn.

"Mommy," Warren whined.

Miss Webster clapped her hands to get everyone's attention.

"It's time to announce the winner of the Fruitvale Thanksgiving Window Decoration Contest."

Everyone got quiet.

Dottie, Casey, and Leon crossed their fingers.

Miss Webster tore open an envelope.

"Third place goes to the Green Grocer for the beautiful display of Indian corn."

Dottie, Casey, and Leon crossed their toes.

"Second place goes to Charlie's Hardware Store. Squanto and Samoset! What a terrific idea."

Dottie, Casey, and Leon closed their eyes as tight as they could.

"First place," Miss Webster said, "goes to Sweetie Pie. I just love the model of the Mayflower. And I especially love the pinecone turkeys!"

The three friends opened their eyes.
Everyone was clapping and smiling.

Dottie, Casey, and Leon jumped up and
clapped, too.

The three friends were still smiling as
they walked home from the feast.

"There's just one thing I want to know,"
Dottie said.

"What's that?" Casey asked.

"When Miss Webster asked what we
were thankful for, what did you think
about?"

Dottie, Casey, and Leon looked at one
another. Then their smiles got even bigger.

They knew they were all thankful for the
same thing. They were thankful to have
such good friends.

The Monthly Calendar

~~~~~~ Issue Two • Volume Two ~~~~~~

NOVEMBER

Publisher: Casey Calendar
Editor: Dottie Plum
Fact Checker: Leon Spector

Jewelry Missing in Fruitvale!

The big news in Fruitvale this November was the opening of PET ME, a new pet store that had dogs, cats, and birds smiling all around town.

But no one was smiling when jewelry started disappearing!

Calendar Club Members Casey Calendar, Dottie Plum, and Leon Spector followed the trail of missing rings and watches to a surprising jewel thief! Or was it jewel thieves?

The Calendar Club helped make this an especially Happy Thanksgiving for all!

DOTTIE'S WEATHER BOX

This November, it rained for 8 days. It was sunny for 12 days. It didn't snow at all. There are thirty days in November. On how many days was it cloudy?

ASK LEON

Do you have a question about a state for Leon Spector? If you do, send it to him and he'll answer it for you.

Dear Leon,

Is there such a thing as a state cookie? Does Massachusetts have a state cookie?

From,
I'm Hungry for Cookies!

Dear I'm Hungry for Cookies,
Yes, Massachusetts has a state cookie! In fact, a third-grade class suggested it! The state cookie of Massachusetts is the chocolate chip cookie. Does your state have a state cookie? If not, maybe your class can suggest one!

Your friend,
Leon